LEOPARDPOX!

by Orna Landau

Illustrated by
Omer Hoffmann

Clarion Books

HOUGHTON MIFFLIN HARCOURT BOSTON   NEW YORK

When Mama went into Sadie's room, Sadie said, "I can't go to kindergarten today. I think I'm sick."

"What's the matter?"

"I don't know," said Sadie. "I just feel funny."

"Do you have a sore throat?"

"No," said Sadie, but she opened her mouth wide anyway. "Aaahhh."

"Do you have a tummy ache?" asked Mama.

"No," said Sadie.

Mama checked to see if Sadie had a rash. She didn't.

"So how do you feel?" asked Mama.

"Weird," said Sadie. A strange cough rumbled
in her throat and turned into a roar.

"I think . . ." Sadie began, as her fingernails grew longer and longer.

"I'm . . ." she said, as her teeth grew sharper and sharper.

"A LEOPARD!" cried Mama. Sadie had LEOPARDPOX!

The little leopard cub jumped off the
bed and scampered around the room.

Mama told her three boys—Gordon, Jordan, and Bannister—that Sadie had leopardpox. "I don't know what to do," she said.

"Why don't we take her to the doctor?" said Gordon.

"Good idea!" said Mama.

So they took a long rope and tied it around the neck of the frolicking leopard. Then they went to the pediatrician's office.

There were other parents and children in the doctor's waiting room. The leopard was ecstatic. She leaped onto the furniture, knocked the plants over, and tried to munch on the receptionist. The other parents complained. "Who brings a leopard to a pediatrician?" they shouted.

Mama was insulted. "This isn't a leopard. It's my little girl."

The other mothers exchanged glances. They were certain that Mama needed a doctor herself.

The pediatrician rushed out of his office. "You must take that leopard out of here immediately," he announced. "I am a doctor for children, not for leopards."

Mama, the three boys, and the leopard walked out.

"Maybe we should take her to a veterinarian," said Jordan.

"Good idea!" said Mama. So they went to the animal clinic.

An old woman with a cat and a girl with a puppy were waiting to see the vet. "Who raises a leopard in the middle of the city?" the old woman grumbled. "You're scaring my puppy," whined the girl, and she hid behind the bookcase.

The veterinarian was overjoyed. "This is great," he said. "I'm sick of treating cats and dogs. I'm so bored, even a mouse would make me happy. But I've never had a leopard in my office before! I'll examine her right away."

"This is a healthy leopard cub," the vet said. "Why did you bring her in?"

"Because this isn't a leopard cub!" said Mama tearfully. "It's my daughter, who came down with a case of leopardpox!"

"Oh, dear," said the veterinarian. "If this is a leopard, it's a healthy leopard, but if this is a little girl, then she is very ill. I'm a leopard doctor, not a little-girl doctor. Are you sure you don't want to keep her the way she is? There are lots of little girls, but this is a very cute and special leopard."

"My daughter is also very cute and special," said Mama, "and I miss her."

They left the animal clinic, feeling sad. Only the little leopard seemed cheerful, pouncing and leaping.

"I'm not sure they will let her into kindergarten like this," said Mama.

"Wait a minute!" said Bannister. "We can take her to the zoo!"

"Good idea!" said Mama, and they drove to the zoo.

Everyone at the zoo was very excited
to see a new leopard.

They quickly put her in a cage. But the little cub clung to the bars of the cage and started to wail.

19

"NO!" Mama roared.

"A LEOPARD SHOULD STAY WITH HER OWN MOTHER!"

The leopards and the zookeepers were frightened. No one said a single word or roared a single roar when Mama opened the cage, picked up Sadie, took her to the car, and drove back home.

"That's that," said Mama. "We'll just have to cure Sadie ourselves. But how?"

"How about cherry-flavored aspirin?"
asked Gordon.

"Or a shot in her bottom?"
suggested Jordan.

"We could wrap her up in bandages,"
said Bannister.

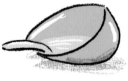

"No," Mama decided. "We'll just be extra nice to her until
the leopardpox goes away by itself."

Mama gave the leopard a big bowl of chicken soup, which she lapped right up. Then Mama turned on the TV. She stroked the little leopard's fur while they watched interesting programs on the nature channel.

Now it was dark. Mama heard a yawn, "Oooouahhhh."
Were the leopard cub's teeth and claws a little less sharp?

"Bedtime," Mama whispered. "Good night."

"Good night," answered Sadie. She still had a few spots on
her skin, but she was a little girl again.

"My darling Sadie!" Mama hugged her tight. "You're better!"

"Yes," whispered Sadie. "But I'm sleepy."

Mama and Sadie snuggled in bed together. "I'm so happy you got over the leopardpox," said Mama.

"But you know what? I feel kind of funny. . . ."

To Yael, my little leopard
—O. L.

To Maia
—O. H.

Clarion Books
215 Park Avenue South
New York, New York 10003

Text copyright © 2012 by Orna Landau
Illustrations copyright © 2012 by Omer Hoffmann
Translated from the Hebrew by Annette Appel

First published in Israel in 2012 by Kinneret Zmora-Bitan Dvir Publishing House.
By arrangement with Kinneret Zmora-Bitan Publishing House, Or Yehuda, Israel, published
in English in the United States by Clarion Books, 2014.

Clarion Books is an imprint of Houghton Mifflin Harcourt Publishing Company.

www.hmhco.com

The illustrations in this book were done in mixed media.
The text was set in 17-point LA Headlights.

Library of Congress Cataloging-in-Publication Data is available.
ISBN 978-0-544-29001-3

Manufactured in China
SCP 10 9 8 7 6 5 4 3 2 1

4500502937